S0-DSE-239

www.enchantedlion.com
First edition, published in 2023 by Enchanted Lion Books,
248 Creamer Street, Studio 4, Brooklyn, NY 11231
Text copyright © 2023 by Matthew Burgess
Illustrations copyright © 2023 by Josh Cochran

ISBN: 978-1-59270-380-7

Printed in China by RR Donnelley Asia Printing Solutions Ltd.
First Printing

for SUE!

SYLVESTER'S LETTER

Matthew Dow

Enchanted Lion Books
NEW YORK

Some letters can't be delivered in the usual way.

But I have a plan:

First, I'll make the skydivers breakfast so they're energized
when I high-five them onto the plane that will lift off

over the ocean and cruise the coastline with its flapping banner

until one by one they'll take the plunge
and form a human flower in midair

all the way to
a squawking jungle.

A river packed with piranhas will carry the letter south to the place where the rare pink dolphins wait,

and when the
moon is full,

that will deliver my letter up, up, up...

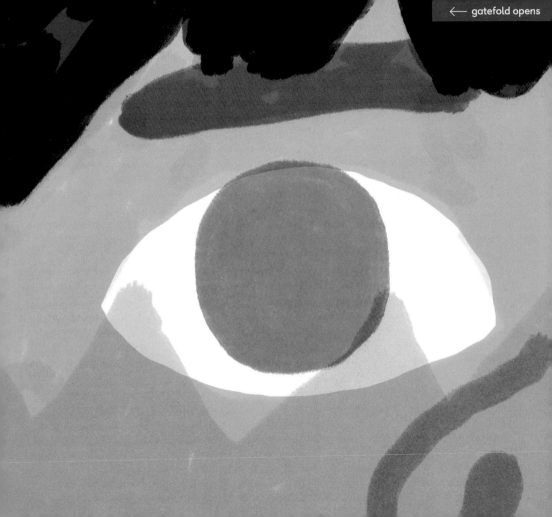
← gatefold opens

gatefold opens $\longrightarrow$

Dear G.G.,
I miss you every day. I always think of you
when Mom puts a pickle on my plate — you being
the most pickle-loving-person I know.

Remember how you taught me the names of insects and birds and flowers and trees? Remember when we hid in the branches of the old Japanese Maple and pretended to be chimpanzees!?
Japanese maple
cricket

You will alway be G.G. to me, but when I look at pictures of you as a girl, I think Georgina suits you too. Your haircut cracks me up!

I wonder where you are now and if you could see me and Mom making your favorite chocolate cake on your birthday. I wrote your name in blue icing and of course we ate it "a la mode."

I was thinking today, that you are one of my favorite people of all time, and the most fun.

I love you forever,
Sylvester